VERITAS MORTE

A SCIENCE FICTION NOVELLA

MICHAEL KINGSWOOD

CONTENTS

ABOUT THIS BOOK

Lucien Bandemyr, Crown Prince of the Qorathi Empite, looked forward to adventure, excitement, and glory from his first campaign outside of the Empire's star systems.

Instead he found frustration, and a betrayal that could bring the Empire to its knees.

Enjoy the book! After you're done, please come to Michael's website and sign up for his mailing list at www.michaelkingswood.com/newsletter-signup/. Guaranteed to be spam free, he uses it to announce new releases and special promotions for his fans.

VERITAS MORTE

L ucien paused before the entrance field to the side-door of his father's audience compartment and straightened his sash, royal purple as befitting his station, then settled his belt more comfortably over his hips. His rapier jangled softly in the quiet of the corridor as he drew himself up to his full height and inhaled slowly. Then, with a quick nod to himself, he stepped forward.

The door slid open soundlessly as he broke the entrance field, and he absently noted two of his guardian drones zipping through ahead of him, their sensors probing for threats even here. You never knew where an assassin may lie in waiting, but it seemed far-fetched indeed that someone would make an attempt on his life in this place. But as his Chief-Of-Staff and Tutor, Abernathy, continually reminded him, complacency had brought down powerful men since before Caesar was knifed by his friends in the Senate.

Lucien tried not to dwell on that bit of cheeriness as he strode through the door, passing two Marines in their cere-monial armor with its gleaming polish and engravings. The two, already standing at rigid attention, seemed somehow to stiffen further as he passed, and they snapped their rifles to present arms in unison. He spared them a quick nod and then just as quickly put them out of his mind as he passed into the compartment.

It was large as far as spaces went onboard ship, but though the ship's designers had done their best to recreate it, the compartment was a far cry from the throne room in the Imperial Palace on Qora Seven. Fluted columns of blue-grey faux stone lined the room from the main entrance to the dais at the end where a replica of the Imperial Throne sat, just as they did back home. But the dimensions were less grand, the filigree less gleaming, the carvings and tapestries replicas. Still, Lucien had to admit it was an impressive sight. Had he not grown up in the palace and gotten to know every twist and turn intimately, he would have no cause to voice complaint. And one reason to prefer this to the real thing.

He raised his eyes to the ceiling, as he always did when he came in here. As back home, it was all crystalline panes, carefully treated to remain transparent despite the lights within the chamber and inlaid in supports so thin it seemed they could not possibly support the weight. But while on Qora the view beyond consisted solely of the blue-pink sky and the myriad puffy white clouds that roved on the whims of the winds, here he beheld creation in all its majesty. There the star field lay, far more dense than could ever be seen planetside, and from this location the halo of the galactic center, where a mammoth black hole sent brilliant beams of light to the far edges of the cosmos, was clearly visible.

It always took his breath away.

"Lucien."

He pulled his eyes down from the stars and turned to

fully face the dais, where His Imperial Majesty, Archibald Bandemyr, Ruler of the Qorathi Empire and Protector of the Chosen, stood with his Chamberlain and a cluster of high-ranking officers of the Fleet and Ground forces. More Marines stood along the wall behind the throne, still enough that the eye almost passed them over without noticing, and Lucien saw Abernathy waiting as well, off to the side. But he paid his aid no mind, instead striding quickly, but not so quickly as to break decorum, straight toward the dais.

The Emperor wore his curly, coal-black hair—so similar to Lucien's own—cut short on the sides and top but long at the back, as tradition dictated. His uniform was white, a contrast with the charcoal grey of his officers' and Lucien's, and he too wore a sash of purple, though his also bore the golden half-moon and star of rule while all others were bare. He wore a rapier on his left hip, balancing a holstered pistol on his right, and his boots were polished to a mirror shine.

"Father," Lucien said as he reached the group of men. He bowed deeply to the Emperor, both hands cupping his heart as he rose. "Forgive my tardiness."

The Emperor made a quick, dismissive wave of his hand that seemed to say, "No matter," but he said nothing for a time. His eyes traced up and down Lucien's body, as though looking for blemishes. Finally, after an interminable pause, he sniffed and gestured toward the officer to his left, a man in his late middle years whose close-cut sandy hair failed to conceal the presence of multiple silver strands in its midst. He had once been lean but now possessed a noticeable paunch, and he wore the pale blue sash of the Fleet over his dress uniform blouse. "Admiral Corrigan was just briefing us on the status of the Corellis campaign."

Lucien's ears pricked up and he could not suppress an excited grin.

The Admiral noticed Lucien's expression and returned it with a knowing smile of his own. "Eager to get a piece of the action, my prince? I recall my first campaign like it was yesterday, why I -"

The Emperor cleared his throat and the Admiral stopped speaking abruptly. He looked abashed for a moment before he regained his bearing and took on a more formal tone. "As I was saying, your Majesty, Task Force Seventeen has taken up blockade stations around Neonovus Six as fragged. Orbital defenses have been eliminated and we now control every jump point in and out of the system. I project that without resupply, the colony will only be able to sustain its defense fields for three weeks at the outside, at which point the Marines," Admiral Corrigan nodded at the burly bald man to his left, who wore the Marine Corps' red and gold on his sash, "will assault."

"How long to take the planet?"

"Two months, your Majesty," the Marine General stated with quiet assurance. "Though as previously briefed we can expect some level of insurgent resistance for a year or more afterwords."

The Emperor nodded. "Very well, gentlemen. In that case - "

An electronic chime rang, and the Chamberlain darted to the side, where a data pad was mounted on one of the columns so as to not be readily visible from in front of the throne. He tapped the screen and frowned slightly.

"The delegation has docked, your Majesty," he said, his falsetto voice seeming to set his jowls to flapping as he moved his jaw. Compared with the military men present, he seemed the epitome of sloth in his billowing blue silk kimono, the fat on his belly and arms swaying lasciviously with every move. But appearances could be deceiving, Lucien knew well. "Minister Ymmersen has made the initial greeting and expects they will arrive within three minutes."

The Emperor nodded again and said, "We will continue this later." Then he gestured quickly with his left hand. At once, the gaggle of men dispersed to their places on the edge of dais on either side of the throne. The Emperor gave Lucien a meaningful look and turned to ascend the stairs to his seat of power.

Lucien followed, taking up station to the right of the throne and a half-pace behind. Then he settled into parade rest.

They did not have long to wait. True to Minister Ymmersen's report, three minutes later a chime sounded from the main entrance doors. A second later, the heavy faux-wood swung inward and a contingent of armsmen strode into the audience compartment in two columns.

The new arrivals wore green and brown fatigues with electroplate armor fastened over vital areas, and bore repeating rifles at identical angles of port arms as they strode into the room. Sidearms and dueling blades on their hips completed their kit and they had the appearance of well-trained and disciplined fighters.

Lucien found himself impressed, and surprised. Capestra had a reputation for prizing peace above all things, and that did not tend to breed a warrior ethos in a people. But if these men were any indication...

The escort stopped and performed a well-timed right-left face, then once facing each other took two steps back to open a path between their two columns. A single voice barked an order, and immediately they went to present arms.

Minister Ymmersen entered the room next, striding briskly between the newcomers until he reached the end of the columns of men. Like the Chamberlain, his kimono was blue silk. Unlike the Chamberlain, his body was lean and hardened from strenuous training, and he stood proudly erect. His black hair and beard were cut short and his dark eyes flashed with intelligence and...irritation?

Before Lucien had time to ponder what had irked the Minister of Diplomacy so, Ymmersen stepped to the side and announced in a loud voice that carried easily throughout the chamber, "Your Majesty, it is my honor to present Her Highness, Princess Ophelia Temisen of the Capestrani Republic."

A faint rustle issued from the sides as the military officers shifted on their feet. Lucien almost lost his bearing from surprise. No wonder Ymmersen was irritated. "Princess?" Lucien said to himself, disbelieving. "They sent a *woman* to treat with us?"

Lucien could just see the Emperor's profile from where he stood, but the sudden frown that appeared there was plain. He glanced back Lucien's way and gave him a hard look. "The Capestrani," the Emperor said quietly, "have some...quaint...notions about a woman's place. Hold your tongue." The last came like a whiplash, and Lucien clamped his teeth shut, lest he say something more.

And then the Princess swept into the compartment and all thoughts left Lucien's mind except awe.

She did not stride so much as float, her movements were so graceful. Her form was long and lean; she was least as tall as Lucien and he stood well above average. Her arms were toned, advertising similar sculpting in her other areas, and though her dress fit the requirements of modesty it did not conceal so much as accentuate the curves beneath. Sky blue, trimmed in white and silver, the fabric clung to her hips enticingly before it fell to the level of her ankles, and on her torso it was just snug enough to show off the curves of her breasts without revealing too much. The neckline was nearly chaste, it was so high; the string of pearls around her neck almost rested on the fabric of her dress. Her hair, black at the roots but shifting slowly to blue-silver at the ends, flowed in lush waves to just past her shoulders and was held back from her face by a silver tiara that was all the more elegant for its simplicity.

And her face. Narrow but not gaunt, rounded but not plump. Her grey-blue eyes flashed with intelligence and poise and her lips were turned ever-so-slightly upward in a knowing smile. Lucien found he could not look away from her, and suddenly his heart was all aflutter.

Princess Ophelia came to a halt alongside Minister Ymmersen and made a shallow curtsy of greeting. "Your Majesty," she said, and the warm timbre of her voice sent a little shiver of delight up Lucien's spine.

If he was not careful, he was going to lose his wits. He forced his eyes away, focusing on the side of his father's face as the Emperor rose and returned the curtsy with a half-bow of his own.

"Your Highness. We are honored to make your acquaintance."

"And I yours." She looked around quickly, taking in the military officers and Lucien at a glance before refocusing on the Emperor. "Your ship is impressive."

The Emperor smiled warmly, "We have worked hard to make it so." At a gesture of his left hand, the Chamberlain advanced from his position. "I have prepared the Empress' suite for your use during your stay. Lord Morsy will show you the way."

The princess inclined her head smoothly. "I wish she were here. I had very much looked forward to meeting her one day, as her beauty and kindness were well known throughout the systems. My deepest condolences, your Majesty."

The Emperor froze for a second, his smile becoming brittle. Lucien was not sure anyone else would have noticed, but he had learned to see the signs of pain, pain that matched his own at his mother's passing, beneath the Emperor's carefully manicured exterior.

He recovered quickly and said, "Thank you," in a quiet tone. Then he drew a deeper breath and added with more of his usual force, "You must be tired from your journey. Please take your ease, and then I trust you will join my son and I for dinner."

Her eyes flicked back Lucien's way, this time lingering for nearly a full second. As her gaze met his, another shiver went up his spine, and he had to restrain the urge to shift on his feet. Her smile changed then, becoming more direct, almost challenging. And then the moment was over, as she looked back at the Emperor. "It will be my pleasure."

The Emperor nodded. "We dine at 1900. Until then, your Highness."

He bowed again, this time in dismissal. She had to know it for what it was, but if she took offense she did not show it. But then, why should she be offended? The Emperor's domain spanned three dozen star systems, while she represented a small planet at the hub of a middling alliance of a half-dozen worlds. And she was a woman, besides. There was no doubt who outranked whom here.

The Princess returned the bow with the same shallow curtsy she had made upon arrival. "Your Majesty," she said by way of farewell.

The Chamberlain reached her side and gestured for her to come with him, speaking softly. As she turned to follow him out, her eyes met Lucien's one last time. And then she was gone.

He swallowed heavily, suddenly realizing he was sweating. Maybe this bit of diplomacy was not going to be so boring, after all.

"WHAT IS your impression of Princess Ophelia?" the Emperor asked, between bites of fruit.

Lucien sat across the table from him in the Emperor's private dining area, adjacent to his living quarters. As with every other space on the ship, it was small compared to what Lucien had been used to in the palace, but by shipboard standards it was huge, especially for only one person's use. The table itself was real mahogany, and it must have been quite a feat to find and preserve. There were not many pieces that could trace their roots back to Old Earth, these many centuries after the Expansion. The table alone was probably worth more than the rest of the flagship.

Well, maybe a small corvette.

Like Lucien, the Emperor was dressed down for breakfast, in a black silk kimono of similar cut to the blue outfits the Imperial Court wore, but as always he wore the half-moon and star over his left breast. He chewed slowly, watching Lucien's reaction to his words intently through his deep green eyes.

Lucien shrugged and stabbed at a slice of melon with his fork, thinking carefully how to answer. They were alone, and there really was no need for caution. Not here, with his own father. But knowing that and changing habits that had been ingrained through years of hard lessons were two different things entirely. Finally, he said, "Not what I expected."

The Emperor snorted out a half-laugh and reached for his goblet, which was filled with the grey-white milk of a Toberian Mollusc Snake. Supposedly their milk prolonged youth and vitality when consumed in moderation, but Lucien had his doubts. The Emperor was not all *that* old yet, and he took a substantial battery of supplements, any combination of which may have kept him looking more youthful than lesser men. Or it may have just been good genes and a healthy training regime.

That did not stop the milk from being outrageously expensive.

The Emperor sipped at the milk and pursed his lips slightly—it was notoriously bitter—before replying. "You expected some wilting flower that we could walk over with ease, eh?" He sniffed and shook his head before lowering his goblet back to the table. "No chance of that in a woman from Capestra. They are uppity creatures, the lot of them." He paused for a moment, pondering. "Still, the Capestrani are far from the oddest societies out here, past our borders." For a second, his expression almost matched the Admiral's from yesterday afternoon. "My tutors did their best, but I was ill-prepared for that reality on my first campaign. Fortunately, Abernathy has proven more than dedicated so I doubt you will have all the disadvantages I did. But there will be many surprises to come."

Lucien nodded, but did not reply. He considered his father's words for a long minute as he chewed on another piece of melon. The Emperor had only rarely spoken so openly of his own boyhood before. Why the reminiscing at this particular time? Did it mean something in particular or...

"I'd like you to spend some time with her," said the Emperor as he wiped his mouth with his napkin. "After this morning's meeting, see if she would be amenable for tea, or whatever catches your fancy."

Lucien blinked, surprised. "I will, father, but...why - "

"It is not enough that I ask it of you?"

Lucien closed his mouth quickly. Too quickly, as his teeth met each other jarringly, with an audible CLACK that seemed to echo through the room.

The Emperor cocked his head to the side as he regarded his son for a second, then he chuckled and smiled, ever so slightly. "If the negotiations do not go well, Capestra and her allies may decide to push the Corellis issue further than is wise. It could lead to an expansion of the war."

"So? We more than outnumber them."

The Emperor's smile grew slightly, becoming amused. "True. But it is not wise to resort to force if it is not necessary. The Capestrani Republic could make a valuable addition to our Empire, or at least a worthwhile client state. If we were to go to war with them, it could make their integration...more difficult."

Lucien frowned. This was an unexpected turn. The Empire had been pushed into the Corellis campaign by Corellis' aggression against Qora's ally. The jump from there to the annexation of Capestra seemed flimsy at best. He was about to say as much, but the Emperor continued on.

"It could be," he said, dropping his napkin and standing up, "that the only way to avoid that will be to form an alliance between our families. If that should be required, better that you and she had gotten to know each other a bit beforehand, hmm?" He pulled on the bottom hem of his kimono, settling it more properly on his shoulders, then turned toward the door.

Lucien jerked back in his seat, as though slapped. The Emperor could not have meant... No, that was... Was it? He called out to his father's retreating back, "You mean to marry me off to her?"

The Emperor stopped and half-turned, an eyebrow rising as he regarded his son. "You cannot tell me the idea does not appeal to you, not after the way you were looking at her last night. She is a comely lass." His gaze hardened as he saw the look of dismay on Lucien's face, and he made a soft tsk-ing sound. "Come now, Lucien. This is how the universe works. Your sister's marriage to Count Poterick guaranteed Heaven's Gate's merger with the Empire, and with them four other worlds. If marrying you to Ophelia can accomplish the same with Capestra and avoid unnecessary expense and death in the process..." He let the rest go unsaid.

Lucien did not know how to respond. Ophelia was attractive, certainly. More than attractive. But not a Lady. Not the sort the Prince—the future Emperor, may that day be far off—ought to marry, anyway. He shook his head in denial.

The Emperor's smile faded completely, his face hardening. "You are my son, Lucien. And more than that, you are the son of the Empire. You belong to the Empire as much as she belongs to you, and you will do your duty for her." He glanced at the wall to Lucien's right, where a ship's status panel displayed, among other things, the local time. "The morning briefing is in forty-five minutes. See that you are on time."

And then the Emperor left the room.

LUCIEN ADJUSTED HIS UNIFORM BLOUSE—HE had changed into more formal attire for the morning briefing, and it seemed fitting to remain thus for the Princess—and drew himself erect, then placed his palm on the call box next to the door to the Empress' suite.

And waited.

The seconds stretched by until nearly a full minute had passed before, finally, a soft chime sounded in the hallway and the suite's door slid open. Lucien blinked, surprised to see Lord Morsy on the other side. The flabby Chamberlain gave a start and took a half-step back, his eyes widening.

"My Prince, what - " he began, but Princess Ophelia's voice cut him off.

"Prince Lucien," she said, appearing from behind Lord Morsy and wearing that same knowing smile she had worn in the throne room, and indeed throughout their dinner the previous evening. "It is good to see you again." Her smile hardened a tad as she looked away from him, toward the Chamberlain. "Thank you, Lord Morsy."

Morsy half-turned to regard her for a moment, then inclined his head, accepting the obvious dismissal. "Your Highness." He managed an apologetic half-smile as he stepped around Lucien into the corridor. "My Prince," he said quickly, then he hurried away in the direction of his office spaces.

Lucien watched Morsy depart and could not help but frown. That was...odd.

"Lord Morsy was assisting me with a matter of protocol," Princess Ophelia said, from very close to Lucien's side. "A... delicate matter."

"Ah," Lucien said, looking sidelong at her. From this close, a subtle aroma seemed to waft from her. Roses, maybe? He did not know his plants very well. Whatever it

was, he had not encountered exactly its like before. It was...
arousing. He shifted on his feet, suddenly uncomfortable as
he felt his pulse quicken. It did not help that Princess Ophelia's smile had turned amused. He opened his mouth to
speak.

"I was just sitting down to tea," she said, taking his words
out from under him. "Would you care to join me?"

Lucien felt himself flushing slightly. "That was my very
thought, Princess."

Prncess Ophelia laughed softly and turned, beckoning
him to follow her into her borrowed chambers. "No need to
stand on formality, Lucien. It's just the two of us here."

He followed her with his eyes before his feet. She was
again dressed impeccably, this time in shades of green,
white, and yellow, but he was surprised to see her hair color
had changed. Rather than black fading to silver and blue,
her locks faded to a silver-green that complimented her
dress perfectly. He pondered for a moment that she obvi-
ously made the change to match her attire, and how long
did that take each day?

He gave silent thanks that he was not a woman, to have
to deal with such trivialities, and followed her into what
until recently had been his mother's quarters onboard ship.

Immediately he saw that Ophelia had not been entirely
truthful. They were not alone. A serving girl stood on the far
side of her sitting room, looking entirely too upright for her
station. There was none of the meek supplication that the
servants in the palace on Qora kept. This girl held her head
up and actually met Lucien's eyes!

Anger at the affront flared before he could stop it. The
nerve of that...that... He forced himself to take a long, slow
breath, to return to calm. She was not of the Empire, and
did not know its proper ways. Capestrani customs were

different; their standards for servants certainly were as well.

"Will you pour another cup for the Prince, please, Deela?" Princess Ophelia asked as she settled down into one of three plumply cushioned chairs that circled a small table to the right, adjacent to the doorway to the dining area.

Asked!

Deela, who wore a simple cream-colored dress that ended at mid-calf and was cinched by a black leather belt at the waist, merely nodded and turned to a serving table, where a porcelain teapot and several matching cups sat waiting. Ophelia gestured to a chair adjacent to hers and by the time Lucien sat down, Deela placed a filled cup and saucer onto the table in front of his chair. He had to admit, insolent as she was, she was efficient.

He picked up the cup and inhaled the tea's aroma. He blinked in surprise. Was that...Earl Grey?

Ophelia's eyes twinkled as she watched his reaction. "When my people colonized Capestra, they brought the plants with them," she said in reply to his unasked question.

Again, Lucien found himself impressed by Capestra. First their fighting men and now this... His father was correct; they *would* make a fine addition to the Empire some day. "I haven't had Earl Grey since I was ten," he said, drinking deeply despite the tea's heat. Burnt tongue be damned, this was too rare a treat to wait on. "My father scoured the Empire but could never find any other sources. That irritated him to no end."

"Then we shall have to see about establishing a trade route, shan't we?"

Lucien stopped in mid-swallow, silently berating himself for letting that slip. Diplomatic negotiations were always touchy, especially those dealing with trade, and letting her know how much his father missed this particular blend would give them—her—leverage. Damn.

"Thank you, Deela," Ophelia said, and the serving girl nodded and departed into the dining room, and presumably the kitchen beyond.

Lucien watched her go and could not help admiring the sway of her hips for a moment. "You give your servant quite a bit of leniency," he said, trying to not let his chagrin over the girl's behavior show.

Ophelia let out another of her quiet laughs. "She is not a servant, Lucien. She is my personal assistant."

He looked back at her, confused.

"She is in my employ, yes," she said, "but she is free to leave my service whenever she wishes, should a better opportunity present itself."

Lucien sat back into the chair, hardly noticing the cushions' embrace in his shock. "What could possibly be better?"

Ophelia just looked at him with that knowing gaze that seemed to come second nature to her, but instead of answering she took a sip of her tea.

Lucien followed suit, if only to get his thoughts back in order. This was not going nearly as well as he thought it would. Swallowing quickly, he changed the subject. "I've read about Capestra," he said as he set his cup back down on its saucer. "Is it true you actually hold elections for political office?"

Ophelia chuckled again and nodded. "We *are* a Republic."

"Yes, but... You are the Princess. Surely *your* position isn't up to a vote of the *people*."

Ophelia's smile faded, her expression becoming deadly serious. "We serve at the pleasure of the populace, yes. It has always been this way on Capestra, and if my family ever does something to warrant the people's sufficient displeasure, they will elect another family to lead in our stead. It has happened before."

"And you would allow that?" That was beyond foolish. That was...mad. Though he knew better than to say as much.

"You cannot understand this, growing up as you have." She actually managed to make that sound disparaging. Lucien opened his mouth to reply, but she continued right on through, trampling his response. "*Legitimate* governments," she put special emphasis on those words, "exist to secure the rights of the people, nothing more. We will have nothing to do with petty despots. On Capestra, and throughout our Republic, we view such structures with the contempt they deserve." Her eyes bored into him as she spoke, and Lucien found himself wanting to squirm in his seat.

But hot anger prevented him from doing so. He clenched his jaw and leaned forward, fixing the Princess with a hard look of his own. "And what precisely do you mean by that, *Princess*?" He intentionally threw the honorific at her, reinforced with all the disdain that her silly platitudes deserved.

The Princess' eyes flared and she replied with heat equal to Lucien's own. "You know well what I mean, or you should. Your *Empire*," she leveled all manor of contempt onto the word, "has been gobbling up star systems for decades, and never mind the desires of their inhabitants. And now you turn your greedy eyes onto Corellis and its colonies, and you expect to just get what you want, yet again. Well, you have another thing - "

A discordant chime sounded, and the wall panel to their left flashed red. An alert. Here, in neutral space? What could be happening?

A 1MC announcement broke through Lucien's suddenly whirling thoughts. "Command Staff, to the Situation Room."

He leapt up from the chair, not noticing the teacup break against the floor as he knocked it off the table in his haste. "Excuse me," he said, only remembering at the last minute to at least put on the required niceties before he departed the Empress' chambers at a dead run.

For a heartbeat as the door slid shut behind him, he caught sight of a smug grin on Ophelia's face.

THE SITUATION ROOM lay less than a hundred meters down the flagship's main corridor from the Empress' suite, but it seemed to Lucien that it took a year to reach it. He fairly leapt through the room's entrance doorway, just clearing it as it opened in front of him, and slid to a stop, barely avoiding a collision with an enlisted crewman who sat at a tactical console not far from the door before he managed to get control of himself.

Admiral Corrigan stood in the center of the room before the main tactical plot, the Emperor at his side. He was raising a laser pointer at a collection of red symbols when Lucien burst in, but stopped what he was saying to give him a look of surprise mixed with chagrin as Lucien extricated himself from the near-collision.

The Emperor did not comment on Lucien's state, but gestured for him to come over without taking his eyes away from the plot. Lucien hurried to the Emperor's side, straightening up his uniform blouse as he went.

Admiral Corrigan cleared his throat and resumed speaking as Lucien reached the plot. "I cannot explain it, your Majesty," he said. His voice trembled, and Lucien realized the chagrin on the Admiral's face was not for his entrance but for the situation. It must be grave.

"One hundred warships," the Emperor said, his tone deceptively calm and cool. It almost—almost—concealed the cold fury that shone in his eyes. "Where did they come from?"

The Admiral shook his head.

Lucien looked more closely at the tactical plot and immediately understood Admiral Corrigan's chagrin and his father's anger. The plot depicted the Neonovus system, which Imperial forces from Task Force Seventeen had just the day before held securely. Now, the Task Force was a shambles. Half of its cruisers were missing from the display —either destroyed or out of the tactical data link, though even the latter meant they were functionally dead as without the link they could not coordinate with other Imperial units, or determine friend from foe, until within visual range of another vessel. Without that capability, those warships dared not engage for fear of friendly fire— as were a third of the frigates and destroyers that had set up the orbital blockade around Neonovus Six. Of the Battleships, Carriers, and Marine Landing Ships, there was no sign.

In their place loomed a swarm of red-tinted symbols depicting hostile vessels. Carriers, Cruisers, a few Battleships...it was a monstrous force, far beyond anything Corellis or its allies should have been able to field.

"My God," Lucien breathed, not noticing or caring about the blasphemy of speaking thus.

"Indeed," the Emperor said, and took a drink from the steaming cup he was holding. "Admiral, what is the official estimate of Corellis' star fleet?"

Admiral Corrigan swallowed and spoke quickly, by rote.

"Twenty-two destroyers, four cruisers, and one dated carrier, your Majesty."

"That is what I recall as well," the Emperor said, punctuating his words with another sip from his cup. "Why, Admiral, was the estimate so far off?"

The Admiral shook his head again, paling visibly now. "I..." He stopped, took a breath, then continued, clearly working hard to keep the sudden tremble out of his voice. "I do not know, your Majesty. I have queried the Director of Intelligence, but he has not yet - "

The Emperor waved him to silence, scowling. "Send a message to Fleet Headquarters, Admiral. I want the Third and Fifth fleets deployed to Neonovus immediately."

Admiral Corrigan's mouth dropped open. "But your Majesty, those forces are patrolling the buffer zones between the Empire and Marrius Prime and Hazador, respectively. We cannot afford to leave those sectors unguarded."

A servant, garbed in the simple purple-lined white tunic of the Emperor's own chattel, appeared at Lucien's side, bowing low as he extended a tray with another steaming cup toward the prince. Lucien waved him away peremptorily; he could not be bothered by such as he. Not now.

The servant flushed—with anger?—and actually scowled at him before dropping his eyes to the floor and backing away again. Lucien almost didn't notice it, but coming on the heels of Deela's behavior and what followed it in Princess Ophelia's—in his mothers'—quarters, the servant's behavior struck a nerve. He turned to administer some much needed chastisement, but Admiral Corrigan spoke again, and Lucien could hardly credit his words. He looked back at the Admiral, amazed.

"I think it best, sire, if we withdraw our forces from Neonovus in order to salvage what we can of the situation."

The Admiral seemed to have regained his bearing fully, but Lucien never thought to hear such a recommendation from him.

The Emperor scowled ever so slightly. "We will not turn tail and run, Admiral. If we show weakness here, our enemies..." He stopped talking suddenly, a strange expression, bordering between puzzlement and consternation, appearing on his face. The hand holding his cup began to shake, and he pressed the other to his chest.

A cold spear seemed to pierce Lucien's heart. "Father, are you - "

Admiral Corrigan reached toward the Emperor at the same time. "Your Majesty - "

Before either of them could finish their statements, the Emperor suddenly stiffened and collapsed to the floor, his cup shattering on the deck beside him. His limbs began quivering spasmodically, and he began foaming at the mouth.

"Summon the Emperor's physician!" the Admiral shouted as he squatted down next to the Emperor. He took his liege's hand in a strangely gentle manner, his face stricken. "Hold on, your Majesty. Help is coming."

Lucien knew he should act. He should do something. But seeing his father fallen like this, he found himself petrified as fear, anger, confusion, and a hundred other emotions he could not put a name to swept through him. He watched in befuddlement as his father's medical staff swept into the room, shoved the Admiral aside, and took charge. In moments, they had the Emperor on a gurney, oxygen mask over his mouth and nose and an IV in his arm, and they rushed him out to the infirmary.

And Lucien just stood there, stunned. Until slowly,

something else intruded on his consciousness: the aroma of the Emperor's tea, now spilled upon the deck.

Earl Grey.

LUCIEN LOOKED through the plexiglass that separated the acute care clinic of the ship's infirmary from the adjoining observation gallery at his father, limp and apparently lifeless on a treatment bed. All manner of tubes ran into him from machines that seemed to surround him, providing him oxygen, fluids, medication...every treatment the Empire's enormous resources could bring to bear on medical conditions. And none of it did a lick of good. The Emperor may as well have been dead, for all the vitality he showed. Only the slow pulse showing on one of the displays, next to his blood pressure and blood oxidation numbers, put the lie to that impression.

In his memory, Lucien had never seen his father laid low like this, or in any way even close to this. He had always been erect, strong, stern but fair, and, very occasionally, warm. But always strong.

But now...

Lucien sniffed and wiped the beginning of tears from his eyes, then gave himself a shake and drew himself upright. The despair he felt at seeing his father thus—a mirror of what he felt not so long ago at his mother's loss—would not serve him, or the Empire, now. He pushed that feeling down, letting it simmer into anger.

Anger, he could focus. Anger, he could use.

The door slid open behind him and slow, measured footsteps announced another person's entrance. Lucien did not have to look to know it was Abernathy; he would know the old man's gait anywhere.

"The tea was poisoned, wasn't it?" Lucien asked, quietly.

Abernathy stopped to Lucien's right and crossed his arms over his chest. As usual, he wore his formal teacher's robes, grey and blue, trimmed in silver-white, over a body that was still heavily muscled for all it had started to go plump about the middle. From the corner of his eye, Lucien saw him nod.

He knew—without having to ask, he knew what had happened—but he didn't want to believe it. Part of him wanted to think her incapable of such an act, the boyish part that saw through the lens of attraction first and foremost. He drew a deep breath before speaking again, and as he did so he felt that part of him crumble away, perhaps forever.

The pain of that struck almost as hard as seeing his father as he was.

"That bitch did this," he growled, forcing the new pain away and willing his simmering anger to become a bonfire that would sear away all of his heartache. "I want her thrown in irons, Abernathy. Her and all her people." He rounded on his Chief of Staff and jabbed an index finger at him. "And Morsy. Morsy was plotting with her. Take him as well." He racked his brain for a second, then added, "And the servants. I want them all put to the question until they confess. Spare no techniques. I want them singing before dinner!"

Abernathy turned his round face toward Lucien and frowned. It was the frown of disapproval that Lucien had come to know so well when he had not gotten his lessons correct, and it made his ire rise all the higher.

"What?" he demanded. "Speak, man!"

Abernathy scratched at his beard, nearly full-grey now, as was the thinning hair atop his head, and shook his head. "My Prince, you cannot take Princess Ophelia into custody."

"The hell I can't! She -"

"Do you have any proof to back up your accusations?"

That took the wind out of his sails, and Lucien was forced to shake his head in the negative. All he had was her demeanor right before the alert, and the blend of tea that had been missing from the Empire for years. But he knew —*knew*—he was correct. Ophelia had tried to kill his father, and... His blood went cold as he remembered the servant trying to get him to drink the tea, the look of chagrin on his face when Lucien refused.

She had tried to kill *him* as well.

"Without proof, there is nothing you can do. She is Princess of the Capestrani Republic and an official envoy from their court to ours. She, her aids, her bodyguard—her entire entourage—are exempt from arrest and detention by diplomatic treaty. You know this. If you violate their status, it would be tantamount to an act of war."

"So what? We could crush Capestra in a month."

Abernathy pursed his lips at the obvious exaggeration, then shook his head in disapproval again. "And then what? If you break diplomatic ties with Capestra and then crush them, as you say, what message would that send? There are no less than a dozen client systems all around the perimeter of the Empire who would see such an act and wonder whether *their* treaties with us will be honored any longer. To say nothing of newly-annexed worlds such as Heaven's Gate, where, I remind you, your sister lives. That one act could destabilize the entire Empire and uproot your father's life's work, to say nothing of the effect it would have on your sister." He narrowed his eyes. "Is that what you want?"

The anger that burned so brightly a moment ago flickered and waned, turning instead to frustration. Abernathy was right, of course, but... He shook his head in denial. "Of course not. But she can't get away with this!"

"And she will not." Abernathy raised his index finger for emphasis. "*If* she was actually responsible. We cannot know that yet, not for sure. Once we have evidence, you can present it to her father and the Capestrani Senate, and demand her formal extradition. Formal, proper, aboveboard. Be above reproach of the law at all times, my Prince. Otherwise you undermine yourself and the Empire."

Lucien ground his teeth, but again he had to admit Abernathy was correct. But just because he couldn't touch Ophelia didn't mean he was without recourse. And maybe there was another way. "In that case, I fear for her safety, given recent events. Post guards around her quarters at all times, Abernathy. No one is to go in or out without approval and only after being searched."

Abernathy's eyes twinkled. "Yes, it would be a shame if anything were to happen to her. Cannot be too careful with a poisoner in our midst. I'll see to it."

"And the others?"

Abernathy nodded slowly. "It is already being taken care of."

That was something at least. Part of Lucien's frustration faded. Part of it.

Abernathy drew himself up and adjusted his robes, then looked Lucien up and down slowly. "You have a pent-up look about you, my Prince. Shall we go to the gymnasium? A few rounds in the ring would do you some good."

That sounded very appealing, actually. But recreation—even strenuous as the ring would be—did not seem like the proper thing to be doing right then. He shook his head. "No. I must..."

Must what? It was not as though he had any part to play personally in the investigation. The Head of Security would see to it, and Lucien was self-aware enough to know he would just get in the man's way if he tried to participate.

All the same, he could not go. Not now.

Abernathy seemed to understand. He smiled gently and, reaching out, gave Lucien's shoulder a soft squeeze. Then he turned and headed for the door, leaving the Prince alone with his stricken father.

"What have you discovered?"

Torrance Hamberly, the flagship's Head of Security, stood half a head shorter than Lucien. He was lean, and moved in a quick, jerky manner that reminded the Prince of a little bird. But he was thorough and had a keen mind, or so the Emperor had said once. Lucien had never worked with him to know one way or another. Now, though, in addition to the uniform of a Master Chief Master-At-Arms he wore an expression of consternation on his face.

"Not as much as I would like, your Highness," Hamberly replied in a direct, no-nonsense tone. "The servant in question does not appear anywhere in the ship's alpha roster. I took his image from the Situation Room's data recorders and ran it through the database personally. He is not a member of the crew, or of the Imperial staff."

Lucien felt his eyes widening, and he looked aside at Abernathy, then at Admiral Corrigan. "How is this possible?"

Both men looked as flummoxed as Lucien felt. Abernathy merely shook his head. The Admiral's mouth hung open in surprised shock.

The three sat in the Imperial Briefing room, along with the other General and Flag officers in the Imperial entourage and Minister Ymmersen. Lord Morsy, of course, was noticeably absent. Hamberly gave his report from the head of the table near the briefing screen, which was dark, for once.

"I surmise," Hamberly went on, "that the perpetrator inserted himself into the database to gain access to the ship, and then deleted all records before he carried out the deed." Lucien began to speak, but the Master Chief raised a hand and answered his question before he could give it voice. "I have forensic data technicians scrubbing the database now. It is highly unlikely that he could have done this without leaving some traces. My team is very good, your Highness. If there is evidence there, they will find it."

"But you still have not found the man himself," Abernathy said. It was a statement of fact, not a question.

"No." Hamberly shook his head. "But the Captain has ordered the ship locked down. No one or nothing will depart, or be transmitted off ship, without being cleared through my office first." He managed a confident smile. "He is still here," he said with assurance, "and we will find him."

"But it will take time. This is a big ship to search," Lucien said, trying not to let his frustration at the investigation's pace—far too slow for his liking, though in fairness less than a day had passed since the attack—show. "What of Lord Morsy?"

"He remains in our holding area." Hamberly cleared his throat, suddenly looking uncomfortable. "But to this point I can find no reason to link him to this act." *And why do you insist I continue to hold him*, he didn't say.

He didn't need to say it.

"He was in Ophelia's quarters, and looked almost scared when he saw me there as well. Why?"

Hamberly spread his hands. "He won't answer specifics, just that it was business of a sensitive nature and not his to share."

"Discretion," Abernathy said quietly, "is a key trait for a man in his position, my Prince."

"That is one thing," Hamberly replied, "and to be commended. But when it impedes an investigation like this, it becomes...less than helpful. Still," he went on with greater energy and in his earlier tone of assurance, "I can find no evidence that he was involved." He paused for a heartbeat, then added, "Aside from your suspicion, your Highness."

Lucien frowned, indecision causing him to remain silent for a long moment. It really was only circumstance that made him suspect Morsy. Hamberly was right; there was no evidence that he was involved. And yet...

"Of course," Abernathy said, interrupting Lucien's thoughts, "you don't have evidence of anyone's involvement, save this false servant, true? Morsy is hardly unique in that sense."

Hamberly gave a little nod, conceding the point.

Abernathy turned his gaze fully upon Lucien, his brow furrowed. "Might as well arrest the lot of us then, your Highness."

"Be careful of your tone, Abernathy."

The old man just looked at him, and after a moment Lucien looked away, abashed. "You're correct, of course." He drew a breath. "Master Chief, release Lord Morsy. But I want his every movement monitored, do you understand?"

Hamberly came to attention, clicking his heels together, and nodded. "At once, your Highness." His eyes flickered around the room for a second. "If there are no other questions, I shall get back to my duties."

Silence was the only response for a second as Lucien looked around. No one seemed inclined to say anything else, so he nodded. "Keep us apprised, Master Chief."

Hamberly nodded again, then turned and left the room, bobbing up and down slightly as he walked.

Just like a bird.

As the door slid shut behind Hamberly, Lucien turned back to his father's—his, now that his father was incapacitated—advisors. "Admiral, how go the fleet deployments?"

Admiral Corrigan blinked, looking surprised at the change of subject. "Ah," he cleared his throat. "Not yet begun, your Highness. The Emperor - "

Irritation threatened to turn into fury. "I believe his orders were clear, Admiral." And those orders had been given hours ago! How dare Corrigan not act! Lucien drew another breath to calm himself, then turned a level gaze on each man in the room in turn. "Gentlemen, we are going to act in accordance with my fath - with the Emperor's stated wishes. Admiral, I want the deployment orders sent as soon as we adjourn from here, and I want a plan for the counterattack in Neonovus and the subsequent revised campaign for Corellis before the day is out."

Admiral Corrigan opened his mouth to reply, but apparently thought better of it; he simply nodded in acquiescence. All around the room, the other commanders glanced at each other, and Lucien could see their thought processes shifting. Did they all think he was a coward, to fall back where his father refused to?

"After that, begin planning for Capestra."

Eyes widened all around the room. Abernathy cleared his throat. "Your Highness, we discussed this. There is no -"

"Yes, yes. We have no proof of Ophelia's involvement, and thus no causus belli to press. Nevertheless, I do not believe for a heartbeat she was not involved. And if she was her father certainly gave the order. Evidence will come, and when it does, I want us ready to act."

Again, silence was the only reply. Lucien could see most did not agree with his assessment, or with his desired course of action. But agreement was not a prerequisite for obedience.

"That is all, gentlemen."

The men stood and began filing out of the room, Admiral Corrigan in the lead. He had a suddenly-harried look about him, and no wonder. In fairness, Lucien considered that he had just given the Admiral an immense tasking with a very short deadline. But that's why the man had such a large staff, and why his salary—to say nothing of the lands the Emperor had granted him over the years for his service —drew such a bite from the Imperial budget.

Abernathy followed the military men out. For a moment he looked as though he were going to linger, but he merely squared his shoulders and left briskly, Minister Ymmersen in tow.

The Diplomat paused at the doorway, seemingly torn for a second. Then he turned back around to face Lucien and allowed the door to slide shut behind himself. He looked beyond troubled. If Lucien didn't know better, he would say Ymmersen was nearly in a panic.

"You Highness, I'm not sure this course is wise. The deployments your father ordered are - "

"What he ordered."

Ymmersen gave a quick shake of his head. "Issued in the heat of the moment, before he had time to think them through. Admiral Corrigan's objections had merit. If your father had the time to consider them he would certainly have veered from his first instincts. He was always one to temper his impulses with facts and realities."

Was? The word sparked Lucien's ire all over again. "He *is*."

Ymmersen inclined his head, conceding the point. "I implore you to reconsider, your Highness. This sort of action could - "

"Enough! I will hear no more of this, Minister Ymmersen."

He sighed in resignation, but if anything the harried look on his face became deeper.

"Was there something else?"

"I hesitate to bring it up in light of your opinion of her, your Highness, but..."

"What?"

"Princess Ophelia has expressed chagrin at the restrictions on her movements and has asked to see you at your earliest convenience."

Lucien snorted. "She cannot object to our concern for her safety. Tell her - "

"If I may, your Highness, it is not the restrictions themselves, but the manner in which they were put in place. Guards merely appeared from one moment to the next, with little explanation given."

"Well, that would be *your* job."

Ymmersen nodded. "I smoothed it over the best I could. But nonetheless, she desires to meet with you." He paused, then added, "She was quite insistent about it."

"I'll bet she was. I have no interest in seeing her."

"Whatever your suspicions, your Highness, she remains an official envoy. If you - "

Abernathy's argument all over again, and all the more

annoying for how correct it remained. Lucien threw his hands up. "Fine, fine. I'll receive her after lunch, in my father's dining room."

Ymmersen smiled then, with relief? Or perhaps it was just pleasure at finally getting something of his way. "As you say, your Highness. I will pass the word to her."

He turned and swept from the room, and Lucien found his stomach tightening up anxiously. He both wanted to see Ophelia again and detested the entire thought of it. And much as he tried to, he could not get the former feeling to go away.

OPHELIA'S DRESS was black this time, trimmed in grey at the seams and hem, with little swirling designs along the bottom half of her sleeves and below the knees. The jewels at her wrists, throat, and ears were all cloudy-white. Her hair, naturally, was different as well, this time merely going from black to silver-grey to match with her gown. As she floated—as always, the word walk did not do her justice— into the dining room and made a small curtsy of greeting, Lucien was struck yet again by her beauty and poise.

It was hard to remain angry at such a woman as she, but he found he could manage.

"Princess," he said in as smooth and calm a tone as he could. "It is good to see you well."

She smiled ever so slightly, but it faded quickly, replaced by a look of...compassion? That couldn't be right. "Lucien," she said, and took a step toward him. "I'm so sorry about what happened to your father." She reached out a hand to him, her fingertips lingering enticingly in the space between them. It would be so easy to take her hand, let his suspicion and anger toward her fade, and just...be...with her, for a while.

Instead, he pulled out a chair and half-turned it toward her, the way a gentleman is supposed to. "Thank you," he said. "Will you sit? I have servants preparing tea. More of that Earl Grey you gave to my father, since you seem to like it so much."

She hesitated for just a heartbeat and Lucien thought he saw a sudden flash of fear in her eyes, but just as quickly as it came it was gone. She let her hand drop and accepted the seat with a nod of thanks.

But that brief flash was enough. He was sure now. *Got you, you little snake.*

"I wish I'd known you gave Ymmersen a crate of the stuff when you arrived," he said as he took the chair across the great mahogany table from her. "I feel a great fool, being caught by surprise in your chambers." He rapped his knuckles against the wood of the table, and the servants' entrance opened. A slight fellow in white-and-purple hurried through, depositing a cup before him and then Ophelia and filling both from a teapot that he left on the table between them when he withdrew from the room.

She lowered her eyes and cleared her throat, not reaching for the cup at first. "No less a fool than I. Lucien, I'm..." She paused, swallowed, then drew a quick breath. "I owe you an apology. I spoke out of turn, in a heated moment." She half-chuckled and shook her head. "I have never been able to hold back my feelings very well. My father almost did not let me come on this trip because of that. He wanted to send my younger brother; I had to nearly beg to convince him." Her eyes turned back up toward him. "I'm sorry. I should not have spoken to you that way."

That was almost convincing. Almost.

"It was rather...unexpected." Lucien lifted his cup and took a sip. He savored the flavor for a moment before swallowing, keeping his eyes on her the whole time. "Diplomats do not normally begin by insulting the other party's upbringing and his home."

A bit of tension seemed to leave her as he swallowed. Only then did she pick up her own cup and drink from it. Of course, had he wished to poison her, the fact that their tea came from the same source mattered little. He could have simply applied the poison to the cup itself before the servant brought it out; that was a fairly common technique, actually. Had Hamberly considered that in his investigation? A thought for a later.

Ophelia swallowed and made a rueful little grin. "Again, I apologize. You cannot help the way you grew up."

Lucien blinked, surprised that she would go there again. The anger he had been concentrating on maintaining flared up on its own. "Again you speak as though I were raised ignorant of the universe. I'm not some backwater bumpkin, Princess. I had the finest tutors available, and travelled from one side of the Empire to the other before I was twelve."

"But never outside of it."

Her words caught him off-balance. "This is my first journey outside our borders, true. But that is our tradition; the Imperial children never leave the Empire before their eighteenth years." Why did she think that so odd?

Ophelia shook her head slowly. "That is why you cannot understand what is happening here." She leaned forward, her gaze suddenly piercing. "You cannot know how the other nations truly view your Empire, Lucien. How they despise it."

"I think you made it abundantly clear how much *you* do,"

he replied with aplomb, and took some pleasure in the way she flinched in response. She recovered quickly, though.

"It goes beyond whatever feelings I may or may not have, Lucien. There is not a system outside of your sphere that does not feel the same way. Even some of your *client states* would just as soon you were gone the way of Tumon of Centaurus. Do you ever wonder why?"

Lucien snorted, and waved a dismissive hand. "Success always spawns enemies, envious people who - "

"You cannot really believe that."

Lucien raised an eyebrow at her. Why not? He had seen such reactions many times in people. Why not expect the same from nations as from individuals?

Ophelia sighed and shook her head. "When over the course of many years, you see friends and allies subjugated one by one, you will naturally wish to see the one who destroyed them punished. That is not envy, Lucien."

Why had he earlier found it difficult to be angry with her? "We destroy no one, Princess. Systems who enter the Empire are built up, given the benefits of trade and Imperial protection, improved infrastructures, law and order... Not a one of them is worse off for having come into our fold."

"Better off, you say." She stared hard into his eyes. "I know of no fewer than three rebellions in the last decade alone."

"Quick to start and just as quick to put down. You cannot claim you do not have your own malcontents." This was quickly becoming tiresome. He set his teacup down on the table and leaned forward. "What do you want?"

Ophelia cocked her head to the side for a moment as she considered him. Before speaking, she took another sip of her tea. "I want peace, Lucien. I came to implore your father to stop his aggression in Corellis, and let his neighbors live without interference."

She had a strange notion of aggression, if she thought Qora was the one who instigated hostilities with Corellis. But just then he realized he had neither desire nor patience to debate with her. "I see." He pushed his chair back and stood up. "I'm sorry to disappoint you."

He turned to leave. Normally he would have been the one to dismiss her, but he just wanted this encounter to end.

"Lucien, wait."

He didn't want to, but he found he could not deny her. The way she said that was...warm...full of need. It made his knees go all wobbly. He had to draw a deep breath to keep his voice level. "What?" He looked back over his shoulder at her. She gazed at him with wide eyes that seemed, for the first time, genuine.

"Your father pursued a path of conquest, but you don't have to. Now that he's - "

He rounded on her, clenching his fists at his sides to avoid lashing out with anything besides his tongue. "Don't talk that way about him, Princess. He's not dead!"

"Yet." She said it calmly, but not without warmth and compassion. "But how long can he last? I'm told he is in a deep coma, despite your doctors' best efforts."

Lucien nodded.

"And *if* he recovers, will he be the man he was?"

He did not trust himself to speak at first. All the anger that he had been holding toward her faded beneath heartache as her words brought his father's condition fully back into his mind. He had pushed it aside beneath thoughts of the investigation, the reinforcement of Neonovus...and his surety of her involvement in the assassination attempt. But she was correct; the doctors could not name the compound that had been used to fell his father. It was a toxin they had never encountered, but it attacked the nervous system, and it seemed to have severe degenerative effects. Even if the Emperor survived his ordeal, they were fairly sure he would lose most of his faculties.

But Ophelia did not need to know that.

"We shall see."

She smiled a sad little smile. "We shall." She rose from her chair and stepped around the table to stand in front of Lucien, and once more her scent flooded into his nostrils. It was different this time, more musky. And all the more exciting for its difference. "One way or the other, you will rule your Empire soon, Lucien, and you can be better than the men who came before you. More just, to your own subjects as well as to your neighbors."

He swallowed, but did not reply. He found he had no words.

She leaned a little closer, spoke more softly, in a near whisper. "Promise me you'll think on my words." He felt her breath on his cheek as she spoke, and it was like the heat of a furnace.

And then she turned and swept out of the room, leaving Lucien to collapse back into the chair he had just vacated. He was completely and utterly spent, and could not figure out how he had so quickly gone from having the upper hand to being the one who had been vanquished.

MASTER CHIEF HAMBERLY found him still in that chair twenty minutes later. The Head of Security bobbed into the room quickly and made just a quick little bow; he was practically bouncing from foot to foot, he had so much energy.

"We found him, your Highness."

Suddenly, Lucien joined the bird-like man in being about ready to burst his seams. He sprang to his feet, his musing about the meeting with Princess Ophelia—and the troubling way her final words had impacted him—forgotten in his sudden excitement.

"Where is he? I want to - "

"The morgue, sire."

Lucien stopped abruptly, feeling as though the wind had been taken from his sails. It was good the man was dead, but... "Explain, Master Chief. We needed him alive."

Hamberly inclined his head. "Agreed, but fortunately, his death brought us more than enough information to move forward." He gestured at a wall panel near the servants' entrance. "May I?"

Lucien nodded, and only just then realized that Hamberly was alone. None of his assistants had come, and he had not brought any of Lucien's staff.

Hamberly tapped the screen to life and looked back at Lucien. He must have seen the sudden wary confusion on the Prince's face, because the Head of Security coughed softly into his hand. It sounded a very uncomfortable cough. "I have not shown this to anyone else, your Highness. The reason why will become abundantly clear in a moment."

That was intriguing. And it was not like Hamberly was going to make an attempt on his life. For one thing, Lucien was quite sure he could break the little man in half. For another, above and beyond the omnipresent guardian drones that lurked unobtrusively up near the ceiling, two Marine guards stood just outside the door—a pair of Marines had not left his side, or near enough, since the assassination attempt—and they would rush in at the first sign of trouble. For that matter, they would not have let

Hamberly through without a thorough checking over in the first place, no matter his position on the ship. Abernathy's orders had been quite specific on that point.

Lucien gestured for him to proceed.

"We found his body in a storeroom near the port side hangar deck. He had been dead for approximately ten hours when we found him."

"So whoever hired him disposed of him once the deed was done."

Hamberly nodded. "A not uncommon fate for assassins, sire. Once they have completed their mission, they become liabilities, and so..." He left the rest unsaid, instead turning back to the wall panel and tapping out a few commands. "As you know, there are security cameras in all corridors aboard ship. Replaying the footage from that section revealed this."

An image appeared on the screen. The false servant, now dressed in the uniform of an ordinary crewman, walked hurriedly toward another man in a crewman's uniform. The second man's back was to the camera so Lucien could not make out his features. The two men met in front of a doorway and the assassin said something, then glanced over his shoulder. When he turned back to his accomplice, his eyes went wide and he made to move away. But the other man was too quick. He grabbed the assassin by the throat and struck him repeatedly in the belly.

"A knife?" Lucien looked away from the screen as he asked the question.

Hamberly nodded. "The man had half a dozen deep puncture wounds in his chest and abdomen. Death would have been painful, but relatively quick."

On the screen, the second man opened the door and dragged the assassin's body inside, then came back out with some cleaning supplies—gleaned from the storeroom no doubt—and made quick work of any blood in the corridor. Then he replaced the supplies in the storeroom and strode away down the corridor.

And during that entire time, he never once turned his face toward the camera. There was no way to tell who he was, except that he was of about average height, and fit.

"Clearly he has intimate knowledge of the ship's layout. That corridor is almost completely untravelled during that hour of night; a perfect location for his needs. And there are other cameras at intervals, but he managed to conceal his face in every single one."

Lucien scowled. "How does that help? I thought you said we had more than enough to move forward?"

Hamberly smiled slyly and raised his index finger. "It helps because I know something he does not, your Highness. There have of late been a number of incidents of pilferage from this particular storeroom, so with the Captain's approval I installed a hidden interior camera." He raised his eyebrows meaningfully. "The camera's existence has not been widely advertised."

He tapped the panel again and the angle of the image changed to that of a camera looking down at the inside of the storeroom door from near the ceiling and back a ways. On the screen, the killer dragged the assassin's body into the storeroom and shoved it to one side.

And then he looked directly up at the hidden camera.

Lucien's breath caught in his throat. His blood went to ice as he beheld the killer's face, and then a towering fury obliterated that ice beneath its heat.

"You see why I came to you first, your Highness. I cannot arrest one of his rank without approval."

"No," Lucien breathed. "No you cannot. Where is he now?"

"I believe he is in conference with his department heads at the moment."

Lucien nodded.

Hamberly waited for a few seconds, then cleared his throat. Lucien pulled his eyes from the screen and looked fully at the Head of Security.

"Shall I proceed with the arrest, sire?"

Lucien headed for the door. "No," he said, and Hamberly's eyes went wide with surprise and confusion. "Have Abernathy meet us there," Lucien said before the Master Chief could speak again. "I'm going to do it myself."

"YOU HIGHNESS, I do not think this is wise. Let me - "

Hamberly voiced his objection—again—from behind Lucien as he hurried through the ship's corridors toward their quarry. The first time had been understandable. The second, annoying. This third time...

"Speak again, Hamberly, and I'll arrest you with him!"

Lucien did not look back to see the expression on the Master Chief's face, but at least he did not try to stop him again.

In truth, it was understandable. He was the Head of Security, after all, and he must feel Lucien was stepping on his authority, perhaps even undermining it. But understandable as it was, Lucien was having none of it. The man behind his father's attempted assassination was found, and he was going to see him brought to heel!

They turned right and nearly ran into Abernathy, who entered the adjoining corridor from the other direction. The old man was breathing heavily—he must have run from his offices to make it here so quickly—and wore an expression of mixed concern and confusion.

"My Prince, what is happening?" Abernathy asked, but Lucien did not answer, just gestured for him to follow along.

There, the door was just ahead on the left. He picked up the pace, eagerness for the confrontation overriding his sense of decorum as he passed startled crew members, who pressed aside to give way.

Behind him, he heard Abernathy speak. "What is going on?"

"Lord Falroth," Hamberly said, sounding almost frantic, "you must stop him! He's going to - "

Then Lucien was through the door and into the conference room beyond.

The table was sized for a dozen men, and every chair was full except for the one at the head of the table nearest the door. All eyes turned toward him, registering varying degrees of surprise as he burst in.

Minister Ymmersen rose from his chair at the opposite head of the table, his eyes widening as well. "Prince Lucien. What can we do for - "

Lucien stalked past Ymmersen's underlings in their chairs, barely noticing them. He had only eyes for the man himself. "You almost got away with it."

Ymmersen's eyes narrowed and he looked from Lucien to the men with him. "Your Highness, I don't know - "

"Enough! I know what you did, and I have proof."

Behind him, Abernathy and the Master Chief spoke at the same time.

"My Prince, wait - "

"Sire, no!"

Lucien paid them no heed, pressing home his victory. "You worked to undermine the Corellis campaign from the start. You never wanted it to move forward, but you lost out. We were going ahead, with or without you. So you decided on another way. You hired a man to put poison into my father's cup, and then when the job was done, you eliminated him." He smiled, his fury at the man becoming an exultant sense of triumph as he laid it all out. "But you were sloppy, and we found out the truth." Lucien drew a deep breath and said firmly, "Baron Horace Ymmersen, you are under arrest for Treason and Murder." Speaking over his shoulder, he said, "Master Chief, take him into custody."

No one moved. No one said a word.

Then, Ymmersen began to laugh.

Lucien blinked. That wasn't how he was supposed to react. He looked back at the Master Chief and Abernathy. Both wore similar expressions of chagrin. What was Hamberly waiting for?

"Master Chief, I said take him into custody."

Hamberly's expression turned sickly and he spread his hands helplessly, saying nothing.

Ymmersen kept on laughing.

Abernathy looked pained. "My Prince, you do not realize what you have done."

"Of course he doesn't," Ymmersen said, pausing to wipe tears of mirth from his eyes. "He was never very bright, or you were never a very good teacher. I could never decide which." He shot a glare of contempt at Abernathy for a second before he turned that same glare onto Lucien. "Let me see if I can enlighten you, Prince Lucien. You are not a deputized officer of the law. You are a member of the Imperial Court. As am I. As is Lord Tutor back there, and several others at this table. You could have opted to let the law of the land handle it, but instead you chose to come as a Peer. Thus, it is a Court matter, and the Master Chief cannot intervene." He drew himself up and sneered at the Prince. "Very well then. As a Peer, I say that your accusation is baseless slander. And seeing as I have several members of the Court who can act as witnesses to this affront, I demand the right of Veritas Morte."

Hamberly gasped.

Veritas Morte. Truth through death. What did that old custom have to do with this?

"Preposterous," Lucien said. "I'm not fighting a duel with you." He looked back at the Marines, who also had followed him into the room. "Corporal, seize him."

"You will do no such thing, Corporal," Ymmersen said, pointing an index finger at the Marine as though that mere act could freeze the man in his tracks.

It did.

Ymmersen turned his gaze back on Lucien. "Even the Corporal understands, my Prince," he said the honorific with utmost contempt. "Veritas Morte cannot be denied, except by the Emperor himself. And, sadly," his lips turned up into a vicious grin, "he is indisposed at the moment."

And suddenly Lucien remembered, and understood.

Veritas Morte dated back to the earliest days of the Empire, when Noble fought Noble for supremacy over Qora. It became a means of deciding justice among the Houses that prevented outright war, and though it had long since fallen out of use, it remained a legal privilege of the Nobility: the accused could prove his innocence by facing his accuser in a duel to the death, and none but the Emperor could forbid it.

Veritas Morte was why no law enforcement officer was a member of the landed Nobility. They worked directly for the Empire, but were not Peers, so crimes could be tried without having to fight a duel, even if the accused was a

Noble. Over the years, this kept the police forces out of petty politics and focused solely on the law and justice.

At least in theory.

For now, it was enough that Veritas Morte still existed, and Lucien had just handed it to Ymmersen on a silver platter. By not allowing Hamberly to do his job, and since he was not yet Emperor, Lucien had given Ymmersen an out, and he had used it.

Stupid!

Ymmersen's smile widened. "You see now, don't you? Veritas Morte, Prince Lucien. Face me, and prove your accusation with blood. Or recant, and prove yourself the craven fool we've always taken you for."

Lucien was well and truly trapped. Abernathy's earlier words seemed to reverberate bitterly in his ears: "Be above reproach of the law at all times, my Prince. Otherwise you undermine yourself and the Empire."

How right he was.

THE SERVANTS HAD CLEARED out the throne room for the occasion, and now the only furnishing remaining was a block in the center of the room that held two dueling rapiers, points down and ready for drawing. Lucien rolled his shoulders, staring at the block from his position at the foot of the throne's dais and trying not to let his nerves get the better of him. It was a difficult task. He had fought countless times in the ring, engaged in unnumbered duels, but they had all been for practice or recreation, with dulled blades and blunted tips. This was real, and those swords could cut or kill a man—could kill *him*—with ease.

Across the room, Ymmersen was completing his final

preparations. He was stripped to the waist, like Lucien, wearing only baggy dueling pants that were cinched at the waist and ankles. Also like Lucien, he was barefoot. His body was lean and hard, and he bore a number of scars on his torso, the leavings from previous duels. It was said he had fought over twenty, for various reasons, and Lucien knew for a fact he was brilliant with a blade.

Their eyes met for a moment and Ymmersen grinned. He liked his chances. He liked them a lot.

"This is insane." Lucien looked to his right, where Princess Ophelia stood with her assistant Deela. And she was not alone; every shipboard member of the Imperial Court was present, lining both sides of the room so that all could bear witness. And why not? Veritas Morte had not been invoked in years, and certainly no other duel had been fought recently with such import behind it. Ophelia wore the same black and grey gown as before—no time to change, Lucien supposed—and a look of concerned disbelief on her face. "Why are you doing this? What can this... savagery...prove?"

Lucien rolled his eyes. She did not—could not—understand. "It's not how I would prefer," he said, honestly. And why did she care anyway? "But there is no choice."

"There is *always* a choice, Lucien. If - "

Three raps of a heavy staff onto the faux stone of the throne room floor interrupted her, and brought all eyes to the center of the room, where Lord Morsy stood next to the block of swords, staff in hand.

"Veritas Morte has been invoked, and here we meet it," Morsy said in a somber tone that carried throughout the room with ease. The Court shuffled about, and the sound of murmurs and whispers came from both sides. Morsy waited for the murmurs to die down before continuing. "Baron

Ymmersen and Prince Lucien will meet, and there will the truth be known. All will bear witness, and all will honor the outcome." He rapped the staff against the floor again, then backed away from the block to join the rest of the Court.

Lucien drew a deep breath, then squared his shoulders and advanced to the block. It seemed a garden's worth of butterflies had taken up residence in his stomach; it was all he could do to put one foot in front of the other without trembling. Ymmersen followed suit, but he moved with a cocksure swagger. Apparently he felt no such nerves.

They met at the block and each rested his hand upon his blade. Their eyes met.

"You were supposed to die with him, you know," Ymmersen said quietly enough that no one but Lucien could hear it. "But I think I will enjoy it more killing you myself." He sneered and withdrew his blade with a flourish, then stepped back two paces and into en garde.

Lucien could not move for a second, from shock at the man's confession. For the briefest of moments, he thought sure he had an out. Ymmersen had confessed to the crime, that would suffice wouldn't it? But just as quickly that hope died. None of that mattered now. Veritas Morte was in play, and the only truth that could be found from it would come when one or the other of them lay dead.

Ophelia was right: it was insanity. But it was all he had available to him at the moment.

Lucien pulled his rapier from the block and stepped back as Ymmersen had.

From the left, two servants hurried forth. They quickly picked up the block that had held the swords, then scampered back to the side, leaving the floor completely empty for his and Ymmersen's use.

Silence loomed, and the moment seemed to bear down

on Lucien's shoulders like the weight of a hundred men. Was he actually doing this?

"Begin," intoned Morsy, from the side.

Ymmersen came forward in a dash, his rapier flicking toward Lucien's eyes.

He twisted to the side, avoiding the attack, and countered with a thrust of his own, but Ymmersen danced away from it easily.

They circled for a moment, making small feints and probes but neither committing, then Ymmersen came again, this time dancing to the side before coming low with a thrust at the hip.

Lucien parried, but the angle was wrong to get in a counter, so he just retreated.

On it went like that, for several passes. Very quickly, Lucien realized Ymmersen was toying with him, getting a feel for his strengths and weaknesses while baiting Lucien to take advantage of openings *he* wanted him to see. The first of those traps almost ended the duel right then, but Lucien managed to escape with only a small cut on his side.

From then on, he was more cautious.

Of course, that gave Ymmersen the advantage of initiative, but Lucien could not see how to change that. Every move, every feint, every dodge—Ymmersen saw through them all and had a deft counter prepared.

Lucien leaped backward from a particularly vicious riposte, but not before he received a cut to his left pectoral. A fine trail of blood flew from the end of Ymmersen's blade as he completed the cut, landing in a stream of drops across the floor.

Off to the left, Lucien heard a gasped inhalation, and he looked aside quickly to see Ophelia covering her mouth in shock. Some of Lucien's blood had landed upon her servant's dress and face. He hadn't realized he and Ymmersen had come so close to them.

Lucien spun to the side and backed away, avoiding a thrust that Ymmersen sent when he looked at the Princess.

"Did you plan it together," he asked in the same tone Ymmersen had used in his confession, "you and her?"

Ymmersen blinked and paused to glance aside at the Capestrani Princess for a second. Then he snorted. "She hasn't the stomach for such things. She thinks talk will solve all of her problems." He shook his head and advanced again. "Fool."

That was an interesting thought to come from the Minister of Diplomacy.

Lucien retreated, getting back into the center of the room while parrying near-continuous thrusts from Ymmersen. His chest and side burned from the two cuts, and his body was slick with sweat. But Ymmersen seemed unaffected by his exertion, and he kept on coming.

It could not go on this way; sooner or later he was going to slip or tire, and that would be it.

Ymmersen darted to the left, thrusting at Lucien's hip again, but he left his body turned a little too much toward Lucien...

He darted forward and twisted his body so that Ymmersen's thrust slipped harmlessly by, then followed up with a thrust of his own, toward the Minister's solar plexus. For a second, he thought the attack was going to strike home.

But then Ymmersen leaped upward and pivoted in the opposite direction, and something struck Lucien on the back of his skull hard enough that he saw stars. He fell forward, his vision going dark, but he somehow managed to tuck his head into a roll as his shoulder struck the ground.

He came up onto his feet at the end of the roll and almost fell over again. The room spun around him and he could hardly tell which way was which. But he could not afford to stop moving.

So he ran to the left. Or, he tried to run. His legs gave out beneath him and he fell again, this time landing on his side.

Keep moving.

He rolled to the side, and something clinked off the stone behind him.

Finally, he found his feet again and pushed himself upright, swinging his rapier wildly around him to ward off his foe, who must surely be coming.

And sure enough, no sooner had he come fully erect than he saw Ymmersen. The Minister actually was forced to retreat by Lucien's wild swing, and he counted himself lucky.

He gathered himself, his ears still ringing from the blow despite the world's spinning having slowed. He tasted blood, and spat out a mouthful of red onto the floor.

Ymmersen paused, looked him up and down, then grinned and made a quick salute with his sword. The pommel of the weapon was bloody, from where it had struck Lucien's head, apparently.

Then he came again.

The attack was swift and relentless, faster than anything Ymmersen had shown to that point. Lucien parried desperately, but another thrust followed. Then another, and another, and Lucien could do nothing but defend.

Finally a thrust came in that he wasn't able to parry, and Ymmersen's rapier stabbed into the meat of his right shoulder. Lucien heard himself cry out, and his sword arm went limp for a second.

In desperation, he tried to raise his weapon back up to

defend himself, but he was too slow. Ymmersen danced to the side and thrust into Lucien's right thigh.

His leg went out from under him and he collapsed to the floor.

Somewhere, he heard a voice shout, "No!" A woman's voice. Ophelia? No, she wouldn't care if he were struck down.

Pain was his entire being. His wounds screamed out at him, the salt in his sweat making their shouts all the harsher. But worse was the pain in his soul. Ymmersen had betrayed him, taken away everything, and now he was going to take his life.

No.

He pushed himself upward, but he could only reach one knee before cold steel on the side of his neck stopped him cold.

He looked up into the eyes of his father's—of *his*— would-be killer, and Ymmersen grinned in triumph.

"Goodbye, Prince Lucien." He began to draw his sword back, for the killing blow.

No!

Lucien heard himself roar...something. He grabbed at the blade of Ymmersen's rapier with his left hand, gripping it with all his might. The Minister's eyes widened and he pulled the weapon back. The edges of the blade cut into the flesh of Lucien's palm as it moved, but he grasped all the harder and forced the blade to the side. He surged upward, his one good leg pushing him up like a piston as he grabbed his own weapon and thrust.

Ymmersen's eyes widened in shock and disbelief, and his mouth dropped open.

They stood there, two men locked in a deadly embrace, for a long moment, staring into each other's faces.

Then Ymmersen's sword arm went limp and he sagged forward. Lucien could see the tip of his own weapon, now red with the Minster's blood, emerging from his back.

Ymmersen's weapon fell to the floor. Lucien moved his hand to the man's shoulder and pulled his rapier out of the Minister's body. Ymmersen let out a groan and took a halting step away. Then he took two more before he collapsed to the floor.

Lucien just looked at him unbelievingly for a moment. He had been so sure he was going to die, that Ymmersen had won. And now...

But why?

The question surged up within him. The question he had asked himself when his mother passed, and again countless times since the poisoning.

Ymmersen's blood flowed freely from his wound, but he still moved. There was life in him yet.

Lucien stepped toward him, stumbled and almost fell, but caught himself. He forced himself to cover the distance, then crouched down beside the stricken Minister. The traitor. He let his sword go and took hold of Ymmersen's shoulder, rolling him over so that he lay on his back. Then Lucien leaned over so he could look him in the eye.

"Why?"

Ymmersen gasped, but said nothing. His eyes looked past Lucien to the crystalline ceiling, and the universe beyond. Blood that had been trickling from his mouth ran down the side of his face. His breath came in rasping heaves.

All the pain and anger of the last day welled up within him, and Lucien grabbed the sides of Ymmersen's head and pulled the dying man's face closer to his own. "Damn you, Ymmersen," he all but shouted, "why?!"

Softly, almost too softly to hear, Ymmersen, in between

gurgling coughs, said "Si... Sirene..."

Then his breath rattled in his throat one last time and his eyes glazed over in death.

LUCIEN LEANED on his cane and tried not to wince at the stabbing pain as his leg protested his refusal to sit down. He could not afford the luxury, and anyway he felt it would be an affront to not feel his own pain fully here, of all places.

Through the plexiglass, his father still lay in his coma, but he was clearly worse. The Emperor's visage was haggard, thin almost to emaciation. Despite all of the doctors' efforts, he continued to waste away. He had at best a few days left. Against that, the pain of Lucien's wounds were like a candle against a hurricane. He lowered his eyes, the emptiness of impending loss filling him. Somehow, the fact that he had avenged his father was little comfort.

Forcing himself to look away, he turned to face the men with him. "Have you been able to figure out who or what Sirene is?"

Hamberly cleared his throat and nodded. "My technicians have completed their search of the Baron's records, sire. It seems Sirene is the name of his late wife."

"Truly." Lucien looked from the Master Chief to Abernathy for confirmation. "I did not know he was married."

"Nor I, my Prince. The late Baron was a deep well of secrets, it seems."

Lucien frowned, troubled, and gestured for Hamberly to continue.

"Evidently she was from Corellis. They met when he was stationed there early in his career, and wed in secret." He paused as though considering his words carefully. "I surmise he feared his marriage to someone outside of the Empire would tarnish his career prospects."

A not unfounded fear, actually. Ties to an outside nation could potentially place one's loyalty to the Empire in doubt, which would hamper one's ability to advance. But still...

"He can't have been the first to marry from Outside." Lucien glanced at Abernathy, and the old man nodded.

"There are procedures that need to be followed, but it can be worked out. We're not barbarians, after all."

Hamberly shrugged. "Be that as it may, sire, he opted to keep it secret. As the years went on, they saw each other from time to time, and they communicated regularly." He cleared his throat again. "It seems he fed her information about a number of Imperial initiatives over the years, as well."

Which was a polite way of saying he had been a spy. Well, one treason followed another it seemed.

Abernathy cursed under his breath.

Lucien was inclined to agree, but still... "It seems a far jump from spying to assassination."

Hamberly nodded. "There is a clear shift in his writings, starting two years ago. He begins musing about the impropriety of the Imperial plans for Corellis. He especially - "

"Wait. Two years ago?" That didn't make any sense. "The crisis between Corellis and Hotor's Star did not flare up until six months ago."

"Officially, no, my Prince," Abernathy said. "But the preparations for the Corellis campaign had been in progress for quite some time before that. The pieces had to be set, the justifications engineered."

"I'm sorry. Engineered? Corellis attacked Hotor's Star. What could be engineered about that?"

Abernathy looked away from him, his expression

pained. "You were too young at the time to be told all the details, my Prince. Suffice it to say, Corellis attacked, yes, but it was not without provocation."

"You're saying we goaded them into it."

Abernathy hesitated, then nodded.

"Intentionally, to give justification for an invasion."

Another nod, and Abernathy still would not meet his eyes.

Lucien turned back to look at his father, the bottom going out from his stomach. The enormity of the lie the Empire had told to the universe—of the lie his father had told him—struck at him worse than Ymmersen's pommel strike. His head swam and he could barely see for a moment.

"This wasn't the first time, was it?"

Silence. But Abernathy did not need to answer for Lucien to know that he was correct.

"What happened to being upright before the law?"

"We met every legal requirement, my Prince."

"But not the spirit of the law."

Abernathy did not respond to that.

"So we were planning to invade his wife's home. He tried to stop it but failed, so he worked behind the scenes to help them build their defenses. Thus the unexpected increase to their star fleet. He must have hoped that surprise would make us rethink our plans." Lucien found, against his will, that his heart went out to the man. Such a dilemma to endure.

"That appears to have been his plan, yes, sire," Hamberly said. "Until eight months ago, when Sirene was killed in one of the initial incidents that spawned the crisis."

And it all became clear. "He could no longer save her, but he could avenge her. So he devised a scheme to kill the

Emperor. And me. And then..." He could not bear to say any more.

Abernathy continued the thought for him. "And then, as the senior ranking cabinet member for external affairs, he could take command and halt the invasion before it could do any real harm. By the time the Houses decided on a successor, Corellis would be a distant memory, and far down the list of concerns for the new Emperor. He may even have had designs on the throne himself."

Lucien stared at his father, and that emptiness he had felt before seemed to engulf his entire being. It had all been a lie. All of it.

"She was right," he murmured to himself. "We are to blame for it all."

"What was that, my Prince?"

"Leave me. Both of you."

After a brief hesitation, two sets of footsteps left the room and the door shut behind them. Lucien just stood there, feeling his world, everything he had thought to be true, crumble away. At some point, he began to weep.

THE AIRLOCK LEADING to Princess Ophelia's ship opened, and she turned and made a small curtsy. "Fare well, Prince Lucien," she said. "It was a pleasure to make your acquaintance." She was back in blue, with the hair to match. But unlike their first meetings, she did not wear that small, knowing smile. Her expression was reserved, distant, as though what she had seen in the duel put her off to him.

He could not say he blamed her.

He returned the curtsy with a short bow of his own. "And you, Princess." He paused, then glanced aside, to where Deela, Abernathy, and a quartet of Marine guards stood. Then he stepped a bit closer and lowered his voice. "I owe you an apology."

Her eyebrows rose.

Lucien looked away for a moment. "I thought you were the one who poisoned my father, and I was rude to you because of that."

"But you no longer think it."

He shook his head. "Ymmersen told me you were not involved."

"You believed him?"

"He had no reason to lie. He was about to kill me."

Ophelia did smile then, a crafty grin that did not reach her eyes. "He underestimated you."

Lucien shook his head again. "No. He was better than me. If he had not stopped to gloat... But no matter. Done is done, but I treated you poorly, and for that I apologize."

Ophelia inclined her head to him. "Apology accepted."

"Good." He stepped back again and raised his voice. "I have learned some things recently. Troubling things. And until I fully get to the bottom of them, I am calling off the campaign in Corellis. The order went out this morning." He tried to manage a smile. "You can tell your father you were successful in your mission."

Her eyes widened, in surprise he thought at first, then in pleasure. "I am happy to hear it." She paused, then smiled, more warmly than she had in days. "Thank you, Lucien."

"I didn't do it for you."

She nodded. "I know. I thank you anyway."

They stood there for a long moment, just looking at each other. Lucien found, as he always did, that he could probably spend an eternity soaking up her features and never grow bored of the sight.

A softly-cleared throat brought him back to reality. He glanced over to where Abernathy stood looking impatient, and felt his cheeks flushing from embarrassment.

"Well," Lucien said, "I hope we will meet again, Princess."

"I think that can be arranged. Until then, your Highness." She gave him one of those knowing smiles, then she turned and strode into her ship. Deela followed, but she took a moment to look him up and down and roll her eyes slightly before she stepped through the door.

The airlock door slid shut, and Lucien could not help chuckling.

"A most interesting young lady," Abernathy observed.

"That she is," Lucien said. "That she is."

"In her own way, I think she is more deadly that Baron Ymmersen ever could have hoped to be." Abernathy looked sidelong at him. "Be careful you do not get taken unawares, my Prince."

Lucien felt his mirth fading, and he nodded agreement. She was one to be handled carefully, for sure. It would be a good handling, though. But that was a thought for another day. Romance, or whatever it was between the two of them, could wait. He had an Empire to set right.

He turned and limped from the room. "Summon the high council, Abernathy," he said over his shoulder. "We have work to do."

"As you command, my Prince."

And so he set off to remake the Empire. His father had built it upon duplicity and conquest, but he would see it become a nation that acted with honesty and honor. And maybe even something a republican-minded Princess could approve of.

There were worse goals to have.

MESSAGE FROM THE AUTHOR

Thank you for reading my book. I hope you enjoyed reading it as much as I enjoyed writing it.

Every review helps an author out, so whether you loved this book, hated it, or something in between, please take a minute to tell other readers what you thought. All of the online retailers make it very easy to do, and I would really appreciate it.

Feel free to come say hi at my website or on Facebook. I always enjoy hearing from readers, especially since you all are, collectively, my boss.

I also have a weekly podcast, Story Time With Michael Kingswood, where I read stories and talk through some of the latest goings on in my world. I'd love to see you there.

Thanks again. My best to you and yours.

Warm Regards,
Michael Kingswood

MAILING LIST

If you enjoyed this book and would like word on new releases and special deals from Michael Kingswood, sign up for his newsletter on his website. Guaranteed to be spam-free, you can opt out at any time. And you can rest assured he will not share your information with anyone, for any reason.

https://michaelkingswood.com/newsletter-signup/

.

SUPPORTING PATRONAGE

Michael would like to invite you to become a supporting member of his website. Similar in concept to Patreon, a few dollars a month will give you access to exclusive content, and help him to focus more of his time to writing fun and exciting stories for your enjoyment.

Sign up at his website:

https://www.michaelkingswood.com/membership/
supporting-patronage/

ABOUT THE AUTHOR

Michael Kingswood is 20-year veteran of the US Navy submarine force and a lifelong fan of science fiction and fantasy literature. His work has appeared in numerous collections and anthologies, to include the Fiction River Anthology series from WMG publishing. He holds a bachelors degree in Mechanical Engineering as well as a Master of Engineering Management and a Master of Business Administration. He has four children and currently resides in San Diego.

Find Michael Kingswood online at:

www.michaelkingswood.com

www.facebook.com/michael.kingswood

steemit.com/@michaelkingswood

MORE BOOKS BY MICHAEL KINGSWOOD

Glimmer Vale Chronicles

Glimmer Vale

Out-Dweller

Tollard's Peak

Robbed Blind

Wedding Gifts: A Glimmer Vale Chronicles Story

The Falconer's Stairs

Glimmer Vale Omnibus Edition #1

The Pericles Conspiracy

Passing In The Night

The Pericles Conspiracy

Dawn Of Enlightenment

Masters Of The Sun

Novellas

What Lurks Between

The Necromancer's Lair

The Champion

Veritas Morte

Story Collections

Tales Of Adventure #1

Tales Of Adventure #2

Short Story 10-Pack

A Jar Of Mixed Treats

Short Fiction

Michael has also published a number of shorter works, links to which can be found on his website.